**Discovering
Cultures**

Austria

Deborah Grahame

 **Marshall Cavendish**
Benchmark
New York

Dedicated to Kimberly Mae and her first-grade students at the Vienna Christian School

Marshall Cavendish
99 White Plains Road
Tarrytown, New York 10591-9001
www.marshallcavendish.us

Library of Congress Cataloging-in-Publication Data

Grahame, Deborah A.
Austria / by Deborah Grahame.
p. cm. — (Discovering cultures)
Includes bibliographical references and index.
ISBN-13: 978-0-7614-1984-6
ISBN-10: 0-7614-1984-5
1. Austria—Juvenile literature.   I. Title. II. Series.
DB17.G674 2006
943.6—dc22   2006011471

Photo Research by Candlepants Incorporated
Cover Photo: Roger Antrobus / Corbis

The photographs in this book are used by permission and through the courtesy of: *The Image Works*: Sven Martson, 1; Eurolufttbild.de/Visum, 8, 42 (left); Rob Crandall, 11; Spectrum Colour Library/Heritage-Images, 14, 43(center); Lee Snider, 18; Topham, 21(top), 21(lower); Shinichi Wakatsuki/HAGA, 22, 34(lower), 43(lower), back cover; Josef Polleross, 28; Oliver Bolch/HAGA, 34(top); Hideo Haga/HAGA, 37. *Super Stock*: Steve Vidler, 4, 42(lower); Yoshi Tomii, 15; Brian Lawrence, 19. *Corbis*: Walter Geiersperger, 6; Derek Croucher, 7; Bettmann, 13; Jose F. Poblete, 16; The Art Archive, 17, 44(lower); Charles O'Rear, 20; Owen Franken, 27, 39; K.M. Westermann, 29; Julie Habel, 30; TVB.BBS Soelden/Albin Niederstrasser/epa, 31; David Ball, 32; Roland Schlager/epa, 33; Heint-Peter Bader/Reuters, 35; Bob Krist, 36; Herwig Prammer/Reuters, 38; Arte &Immagini sri/, 44(top); Reuters, 45. *Minden Pictures*: Tim Fitzharris, 9. *Robert Fried Photography*: Robert Fried, 10. *Index Stock*: Walker, 12, 43(top). *image2d.com*: 24, 25(top), 25(lower), 26.

Cover: *Vienna's Schönbrunn Palace and gardens*; Title page: *A young boy in lederhosen at a festival*

Map and illustrations by Ian Warpole
Book design by Virginia Pope

Printed in Malaysia
1 3 5 6 4 2

Turn the Pages...

Where in the World Is Austria?

Austria is a small country in central Europe. It is landlocked, or shut in on all sides by land with no way to the sea. Eight other countries touch its borders. To the north, Austria shares borders with Germany and the Czech Republic. To the south are Italy and Slovenia. Hungary and Slovakia lie to the east, and Switzerland and Liechtenstein are to the west.

In area, Austria covers 32,376 square miles (83,853 square kilometers). That's just about the size of South Carolina, in the United States.

Austria's tallest mountain, Grossglockner, rises above the Pasterze Glacier.

The country is divided into nine provinces: Burgenland, Carinthia, Lower Austria, Salzburg, Styria, Tirol, Upper Austria, Vienna (the city), and Vorarlberg.

Mountains cover three-quarters of the land. The most majestic of these are the Alps. The Austrian Alps were formed during the Ice Age, between 600,000 and 10,000 years ago. *Glaciers* still stand as huge mountains of ice in the Alps today.

Map of Austria

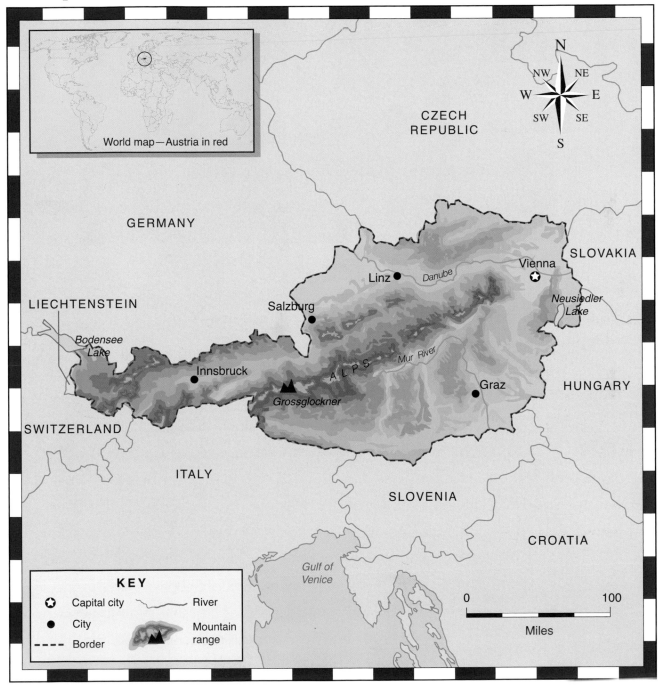

World map—Austria in red

N
NW · NE
W · E
SW · SE
S

CZECH REPUBLIC

GERMANY

SLOVAKIA

LIECHTENSTEIN

Linz
Danube
Vienna

Salzburg

Neusiedler Lake

Bodensee Lake

A L P S

Mur River

Innsbruck

Grossglockner

Graz

HUNGARY

SWITZERLAND

ITALY

SLOVENIA

CROATIA

Gulf of Venice

KEY

⬡ Capital city   River

● City   Mountain range

--- Border

0   100

Miles

Forests and mountains surround an Austrian lake.

Austria's mountains are an important natural resource. They hold treasures such as the metals magnesite and graphite. Other products found in Austria's mountains include iron ore, coal, lead, petroleum, natural gas, copper, salt, and zinc.

Austria's tallest mountain is Grossglockner, located in the Central Alps. It is 12,457 feet (3,797 meters) above sea level. Austria's lowest point is Neusiedler Lake at 337 feet (115 m) above sea level. This lake is warm, shallow, and surrounded by reeds. It is no more than 7 feet deep, even in the middle. It is also Austria's largest lake. The Bodensee Lake forms Austria's western border with Switzerland and Liechtenstein. As Austria's glaciers melt over time, alpine lakes are created.

Rivers and valleys form natural passages through the Alps. Since *prehistoric* times, these passages have made Austria the crossroads of Europe. The Brenner Pass in western Austria is one of the most important places for crossing the Alps from north to south. The Semmering Pass in eastern Austria gave ancient travelers from the north easy access to Italy and the Adriatic Sea. Today, the Brenner Pass has a superhighway, called the Brenner Autobahn, and a high-speed railroad connecting Austria and Italy.

Rivers provide hydroelectric or water power to produce electricity for the country. Austria *exports* some of this electricity to other European countries. Austria's longest river is the Danube. It starts in Germany and runs through eight countries on its way to the Black Sea. It flows 217 miles (350 km)

Cars and trucks traveling on the Brenner Autobahn

through the northern part of the country. Most of Austria's rivers on the northern slope of the Alps flow into the Danube. Throughout the ages, the Danube has been an important river for trade and communication.

Austria has four seasons, each with a different type of weather. Spring and fall are mild. Summer is short, and temperatures are moderate. Winters can be quite cold in the mountain valleys.

As winter comes to an end, winds from the south called *foehns* whip across the valleys. These warm, dry winds can cause snow to melt so suddenly that avalanches can occur. But the foehns warm up the land quickly so that early planting can begin in the southern valleys.

Forests cover about 40 percent of Austria. These provide wood, paper, and other products. Austria has strict laws to protect its forests. A replanting program makes sure that Austria's valuable forest resources are not used up too quickly.

Only about 20 percent of Austria's land is good for farming. Most farms in Austria are small, but farmers use the latest technology to make the most of the land. Important products include potatoes, sugar beets, oats, barley, apples, and corn. Dairy farms and livestock (farm animals) provide Austrians with all the eggs, meat, and milk they need.

The beauty of Austria's natural wonders is matched by its grand cities. Austria's capital city, Vienna, lies on the banks of the Danube River. The soil is rich and the climate is mild. Graz is the second largest city in Austria. It was built on both sides of the Mur River. This city is noted for its fine universities, architecture, and cultural events. Austria's third largest city, Linz, is a major industrial center. The largest port on the Danube River is located in Linz. Other important cities include Salzburg. *Salz* means salt in German. This city was once a

Vienna, Austria's capital city, seen from the sky

center for salt mining. Innsbruck is located where the Sill and Inn rivers meet. This city hosted the Winter Olympics in 1964 and 1976.

The White Storks of Rust

The white stork is one of the largest birds in Europe. It is more than 3.5 feet (1 m) tall with wings that stretch more than 5 feet (1.5 m) wide. Its fluffy white feathers and black wings contrast with its bright red, sticklike legs and long red bill.

The stork has a unique relationship with the people—and the chimneys—of a small village called Rust, located outside Vienna. Each spring in the month of May, the storks return to the same village—even to the very same nest—after spending the winter in North Africa. Since they mate for life, the storks arrive with the same mate, as well. People prepare for their old friends' return by placing wooden frames over their chimneys. They believe that each stork brings good luck to the house where it chooses to build its nest and raise its young. Come September, after the eggs have hatched and the young are full grown, the stork family flies back to its winter home in North Africa. The following spring, the cycle will begin again.

What Makes Austria Austrian?

A smiling young Austrian girl

Austria's central location has put the land at the crossroads of Western Europe. People from many cultures traveled through Austria on their way to other cities and countries, trading goods and ideas. As a result, Austria developed a rich culture that is uniquely Austrian.

Like Americans, Austrians have a mixture of national and ethnic backgrounds. Some Austrians are fair with blue eyes, some are dark with dark eyes —and many are somewhere in-between. One thing that unites Austrian people is their language. German is Austria's official language. It is spoken by about 98 percent of Austrians.

Four boys sit on a statue in front of a church.

German and English share some common words, such as *kaffee* and coffee, *haus* and house, and *gut* (pronounced "goot") and good. Some words, like hotel and sport, look and sound just about the same in both languages. Austrians and Germans have different words for many things, however. In Germany, for example, a tomato is a *tomate* but in Austria it is a *paradeiser*. In Austria a hospital is a *spital*, but in Germany it is a *krankenhaus*. There are also some differences in grammar and pronunciation.

Saint Charles' Church in Vienna

Besides language, many Austrians are united by a common religion. About 80 percent of the people are Roman Catholic. But Austrians are free to practice any religion they choose. About 5 percent of the people are Protestant. In recent years, immigrants have brought the Muslim religion to Austria. It is one of the fastest-growing religions in Austria today. Austria once had a large Jewish community, but it was destroyed in the Holocaust before and during World War II. About 12,000 Jews live in Austria today.

Dr. Sigmund Freud

Austrians have made important contributions to the world in the fields of medicine and psychology. Konrad Lorenz received the Nobel Prize for medicine in 1973 for his research work in animal and human behavior. Sigmund Freud was a doctor who developed important theories about people's thoughts, feelings, and dreams. His influence still can be felt today in the areas of psychology, science, and culture.

Austria's government is a republic. Like the United States, Austria has an executive branch, a legislative branch, and a judicial branch. A president and a chancellor head the executive branch.

Austria's president lives in the Hofburg Palace in Vienna.

The Schönbrunn Palace and gardens in Vienna

The president is the head of state and commander in chief of the armed forces. The people elect the president for a six-year term. The president's role is symbolic and does not carry the power to declare war or to reject laws passed by the *legislature*. The president appoints the chancellor, who serves for four years.

Under the rule of the Habsburg family in the late 1200s, Austria grew into a huge *empire*. During this golden age, the Habsburgs built many of the palaces,

A painting in the dome of Saint Charles' Church

cathedrals, fortresses, and monasteries that beautify Austria's major cities. Painters decorated these amazing structures inside and out with exciting, colorful scenes. Today these buildings are reminders of the former glory of the Austrian empire.

Austrian Music

Austrians are very proud of their cultural traditions. They love theater and music. Many great composers have lived and worked in Austria. Wolfgang Amadeus Mozart was born in Salzburg. Each year this city honors him with a festival attended by people from around the world. Joseph Haydn wrote more than one hundred symphonies and many other musical works. Haydn is known today as one of the founders of Vienna's classical music style. Franz Schubert wrote *lieder*, or songs, and composed piano music and symphonies. His lovely song, "Ave Maria," still moves and inspires people today. Johann Strauss Jr. is known as Austria's "King of the Waltz." He wrote the most famous waltz in the world, "The Blue Danube."

Living in Austria

Most Austrians today live in cities and towns. Vienna, Austria's capital and largest city, is home to about one-seventh of the people. Most people in the cities live in apartment buildings, but some city-dwellers do live in single-family homes.

Many colors and shapes decorate an apartment building in Vienna.

Homes and a church in a lakeside village

People in small towns and villages live in houses. The styles of the houses depend on where they live. Many farmers live in traditional farmhouses that have been in their families for hundreds of years.

Austria is one of the world's most popular vacation spots. As a result, there are plenty of jobs in hotels, restaurants, and gift shops. About one-fourth of Austria's workers earn their living by providing goods and services. This means they work in places such as hospitals, schools, banks, real estate agencies, and insurance

Making a wineglass by hand at an Austrian crystal factory

companies. Another one-fourth of the people work in factories that manufacture some of Austria's main products: cars, tools, ships, trains, and machinery. Austria is noted for its skilled workers and finely made crafts, including Austrian glass, wood, ceramic, and textile items.

Austria is a modern nation. Its citizens enjoy many benefits from the federal government. Older, retired people receive a monthly pension. New mothers are given long maternity leaves from their jobs. People who become ill or are hurt on the job are given disability payments to help pay their bills. All of Austria's citizens have health-care coverage through a national program.

Austrians love fine food. Popular on tables throughout the land are goulash from Hungary, stuffed cabbage from Poland, and *knödel* (dumplings) from

Salzburg dumplings

Bohemia. Dumplings are a part of soups, stews, and even desserts. A specialty of chefs in Austria is *Wiener schnitzel*. This world-famous Viennese dish is thought to have come originally from Italy. It is a thinly sliced veal or pork cutlet that is dipped in egg and bread crumbs and then lightly fried. Schnitzel is traditionally served with cold potato or cucumber salad.

For breakfast, bakeries make a variety of breads, from *landbrot*, a hearty, crusty rye bread, to *vollkorn*, a healthy, whole grain loaf. Adults drink a big mug of half-coffee, half-milk known as a *melange*. Traditionally, the main meal of the day is served at noon in Austria. It often is soup, a main course of meat and potatoes, and dessert. Lunch in a restaurant might be a selection of fancy pastries layered with ham and cheese and painted with a shiny, clear gelatin on top. Little white bread buns called *kaisersemmel* are popular for making cold cuts and cheeses into super sandwiches for picnics. Snack bars and street vendors sell *frankfurter* and other types of sausage served on a long roll. Dinner is light and simple.

Austria has delicious desserts. Pastries are an art form in Austria. Chefs study the art for years, learning to create such masterpieces as *Sachertorte*. This is a rich chocolate cake spread with apricot jam and then with another layer of

Sachertorte served with tea

Children wearing traditional dress, or tracht, at an Austrian festival

dark chocolate frosting and topped with whipped cream. Apple pie and brownies are favorites in the United States. But in the hands of Austria's talented pastry chefs, these ingredients are transformed into treats fit for a king or queen: *apfelstrudel* (a flaky apple pastry) and *rehrücken* (a rich chocolate cake).

Austrians like to wear jeans and sweaters, T-shirts, and sneakers, as do people in the United States. But people in Austria also like to dress up in suits and dresses a bit more often than Americans do. For holidays and special events, many Austrians enjoy wearing their traditional national dress, or tracht. These special clothes have often been handed down from generation to generation. By wearing the tracht, men and women dress as peasants or townspeople did long ago. Men wear *lederhosen*, short leather pants with suspenders, or britches with woolen jackets and hats decorated with a cord or a feather. Women wear a *dirndl*, a skirt with an apron, a short jacket, and a white embroidered blouse. The tracht from each region in Austria has its own distinct designs, patterns, and colors.

Vienna Crescent Cookies

These cookies are traditional at Christmas but are also delicious anytime. They are easy to make, but you will need an adult to help you. Wash your hands before you begin.

Ingredients:

2 sticks ($1/2$ pound)
unsalted butter, softened

$3/4$ cup powdered sugar

2 teaspoons vanilla

1 cup ground walnuts or almonds

2 cups all-purpose flour

First beat the butter until light and creamy. Sift the sugar over the top of the butter and beat these together well. Stir in the vanilla and walnuts or almonds. While you stir, gradually sift in the flour. You now have cookie dough! Work the dough with your hands until it is well blended. Pinch off one-tablespoon-size pieces of the dough and roll into a short rope before forming each crescent, or half-moon shape. Place the cookies on a greased baking sheet about an inch apart, then bake in a 350 °F oven for 15 minutes. When cool, sprinkle with lots of powdered sugar. Makes 4 dozen.

School Days

The oldest schools in Austria were founded by the Catholic Church. Benedictine monks opened a school in Vienna called the *Schottengymnasium* in 1155. This school continues to operate today. A law passed in 1774 provides free education for all Austrians. Thanks to this law almost all Austrians can read and write.

All children must attend school for nine years, from age 6 to 15. Most children attend public school, which is free. Some parents pay for their children to attend

Girls share a desk in a classroom.

A teacher and her students during a lesson

private school. The Vienna Christian School is a private school for children from many countries.

Elementary school is known as *volksschule*. Children attend volksschule for four years. During this time they study reading, math, and writing, along with music and art. Children also learn English in elementary school. In grades one and two, they learn songs in English. In grades three and four, they learn to read and write English.

Reading skills are stressed. Subjects including math, music, physical education, and reading and writing are all taught by one teacher. Students are graded on a scale of 1 through 5, with 1 being the highest, or A.

Homework

Playing a game at school

Until fourth grade, children have a short school day that ends by noon or one o'clock. They do not eat lunch at school, but pause for ten-minute snack breaks instead. Children bring a midmorning snack from home.

Outdoor recess lasts about twenty minutes. Children play tag, jump rope, dodgeball, basketball, and Chinese jump rope.

After elementary school, Austrian students and their parents make a big decision. A student can choose to attend a vocational school to learn job skills, or to attend high school to prepare for college.

Austria has twenty-one universities, including six fine arts colleges and a large number of technical schools. The largest university in the country is the University of Vienna, founded in 1365. Austria also has several fine music schools. The "Mozarteum" University of Music and the Performing Arts is located in Mozart's hometown of Salzburg.

The Vienna Boys' Choir

This world-famous group of singing boys was founded in 1498. Today the choir is made up of approximately one hundred boys in four groups from ages eleven through fourteen. Each boy must audition to become a member. He must have a good knowledge of music and an excellent singing voice. Only the most angelic voices are admitted to the choir.

The boys live and go to school in Vienna's Augarten Palace. Unless they are on tour, these talented boys perform each week at Sunday Mass in the Hofburg Palace. Members of the Vienna Boys' Choir travel around the world. People crowd concert halls and auditoriums to hear this heavenly sample of Austrian music.

Just for Fun

Austria is a first-rate winter playground. The Alps attract winter sports lovers and adventurers from all over the world.

Skiing is the number one sport in Austria. Football (known in the United States as soccer) holds the number two spot. Have you heard of *curling*? This winter sport has nothing to do with hair! Players push heavy stones across the ice toward a target. Austrians even play golf on the ice! The country's only ice golf course is on the Weissensee Lake in the Carinthia province.

Young skiers with their instructor

Waterskiing on a lake

Many Austrian children learn to ski, skate, and sled with their families almost as soon as they can walk. Winter sports keep families busy and fit all year long.

The beautiful lakes and countryside seem to come alive in summer. Austrians enjoy hiking, swimming, waterskiing, fishing, and sailing. People ride bicycles in search of the perfect picnic spot. Recently, mountain biking has become very popular in Austria. Mountain climbing and long-distance hiking are also favorite

Mountain biking in Tirol

sports. Trails are well marked and adventurers can stop at special huts throughout the mountains for meals and shelter.

Austrians love nature and the outdoors. Hikers, animal lovers, birders, and adventurers visit the Hohe Tauern National Park. A major attraction there is Austria's highest peak, Grossglockner. There are approximately three hundred mountain peaks throughout the park. Visitors can climb stairs leading to the Pasterze Glacier. They can take a cable car ride to experience awesome views.

Austrians can even tour inside a mountain mine! Celts mined for salt back in the time of the ancient Romans. The mines are now lit for today's explorers. People can ride the mining cars and even toboggan down chutes made of tree trunks as they go deep into the mines.

After all that exercise, it's time for a rest! Coffeehouses are where Austrians meet and greet each other.

Tourists take a cable car ride through the mountains.

Students, shoppers, and office workers can be seen there any time of day. They like to relax with coffee and a sandwich or pastry while playing cards or chess or reading a newspaper. Some people shop to relax. Street markets, flea markets, and fairs take place on weekends in cities, towns, and villages across the country. Austria's biggest street market is the *Naschmarkt* in Vienna. Each market stall offers a specialty: flowers, fruits and vegetables, pottery, glassware, clothing, or fresh baked treats.

Vienna's Prater Park is Austria's playground. It was once the emperor's private hunting park. People today visit the park to jog, ride bicycles, and hold soccer games. Families can ride the giant 212-foot (65 m) Ferris wheel, or climb aboard the roller coasters and merry-go-rounds. This park is a green natural beauty in the midst of Vienna's steel and stone structures. It can be compared to New York

The giant Ferris wheel in Prater Park

City's Central Park. The Vienna Woods is another peaceful setting that Austrians and their visitors enjoy.

The city's palaces and museums are lovely to look at from the street, but they also hold amazing *artifacts* inside. Beneath Saint Stephen's Cathedral are *catacombs*, or burial mazes, that hold thousands of skeletons. The Hofburg Palace has a fine collection of weapons and armor. The palace is also home to an extraordinary horse-riding school.

The Spanish Riding School

Horses are prized in Austria for their grace as well as their speed and strength. Some of the world's most graceful horses perform at Vienna's *Spanische Reitschule* (Spanish Riding School) in the Hofburg Palace. What are Spanish horses doing in Austria? The art of training horses to do complicated exercises came from Spain. The horses themselves, known as Lipizzaners, were originally brought to Austria from Lipizza in Slovenia.

These horses—and their riders—are specially trained for many years to perform careful, fancy movements. They practice steps once used in battle by Austrian soldiers more than five hundred years ago. Horses and riders wear embroidered saddles and fancy uniforms. The Lipizzaners weave and prance for thrilled audiences who wait months for tickets to the spectacular eighty-minute show.

Let's Celebrate!

Austrians value their traditions. Religious holidays such as Easter and Christmas are central to many celebrations in this mostly Roman Catholic country.

Austrian festivals are rich in history. Some began hundreds of years ago. For example, in February people in the province of Tirol dress up in scary masks and carry long sticks to chase away the evil spirits of winter during *Fasching*. They march through the streets in costume while waving the sticks in the air. This tradition goes back to ancient times.

Wearing a witch's mask for a Fasching celebration

Fasching is a joyous time that lasts from New Year's Eve until Ash Wednesday, when the holy season of Lent begins. It is similar to Mardi Gras in New Orleans and Carnival in South America, when people go a bit "crazy." In Austria, people attend grand balls and pageants or dress up in costumes and masks. There are about three hundred balls that take place in Vienna during Fasching.

Children dressed in costumes during Fasching

May Day festivities in Vienna

Easter is called *Oster* in Austria. Holy Week, the week before Easter, is a time for passion plays. In these plays, actors bring to life the last days of Jesus Christ. On the night before Easter, bonfires are lit on many mountain slopes. On Easter morning, children awake to the fun of a chocolate Easter egg hunt.

Austrians observe civic holidays similar to those celebrated by Americans. *Tag der Arbeit*, or Labor Day, falls on May 1. It is a day for workers' demonstrations, marches, and sporting events. National Day in Austria is October 26. It is a day when all citizens express pride in their country.

In summer there seems to be a festival of every kind across the land. The Salzburg Festival features concerts, plays, and special performances, such as the Fire Dance, in Mozart's honor. It is one of Europe's most important musical events. There is a Dumpling Festival in the city of Saint Johann and a giant chocolate festival in Bludenz. The International Summer Dance Festival lasts for two weeks each July in Innsbruck. Wine festivals take place throughout Lower Austria.

Saint Martin's Day is November 11. All of Austria feasts on *Martinigans*, or roast Saint Martin's goose. This meal honors Saint Martin of Tours, a Catholic saint. In late November

People shop in an open-air Christmas market in Graz.

Nikolo and Krampus visit children on Saint Nicholas Day.

the *Weihnachtsmärkte* (Christmas market) season begins and lasts until late December. Tree decorations, food and drink, and gifts are available at open-air markets in all cities.

Throughout Austria, Christmas is filled with folk traditions. *Nikolo*, as Saint Nick, or Santa Claus, is called in Austria, visits children on Saint Nicholas Day, December 6. Nikolo is often accompanied by a devil called *Krampus*, who reminds children to be good.

Advent is a time of waiting for the Christ Child. Advent concerts fill the air in Salzburg. In the province of Tirol, churches and homes display nativity scenes that represent the birthplace of Christ in a stable.

At Christmas, Austrians eat a traditional meal of fish or roast goose with dumplings and red cabbage. On

The Vienna Philharmonic Orchestra performs at the New Year's concert.

New Year's Day, or *Neujahr*, Austrians celebrate by dancing in the streets and drinking champagne while fireworks fill the sky. Austrian National Television broadcasts the Vienna Philharmonic Orchestra's traditional New Year's concert to radio and TV stations around the world.

In some ways, the Austrian way of life is itself a celebration. The national passion for art, music, sports, and fine food bring beauty, fun, and happiness to life each day of the year.

"Silent Night"

Austria gave the world a musical Christmas gift in 1818. The beloved carol "Silent Night" was written on Christmas Eve that year, in the Austrian village of Oberndorf. Some say hungry mice ate through the church organ belt that winter. This meant no organ music for the Christmas Eve service! The pastor and choirmaster quickly composed a simple song, accompanied by a guitar. Today, "Silent Night" is one of the most popular Christmas carols of all time.

Austria's flag is made up of three horizontal stripes of equal width. In the center is one white stripe with a red stripe above and below. Legend says that the design was inspired by Austrian Duke Leopold V. He died a hero in battle in 1191, his clothing soaked bright red with blood except for the part under his belt, which stayed white.

Austria uses the euro as its national currency. In May 2006, one euro equaled about $1.28 in the United States.

Count in German

English	German	Say it like this:
one	eins	eyns
two	zwei	tsvigh
three	drei	dry
four	vier	feer
five	fünf	fuenf
six	sechs	zeks
seven	sieben	ZEE-bin
eight	acht	akht
nine	neun	noin
ten	zehn	tsane

Glossary

artifacts (AR-ti-fakts)   Objects such as tools or pottery made by people long ago.

catacombs (KA-tuh-kohms)   An underground cemetery with passageways for tombs.

curling (KUHR-ling)   A sport in which two teams of four players slide a stone over ice toward a target.

empire (EM-pire)   A group of lands or countries under the control of one ruler.

export (EX-port)   To send goods to other countries to be traded or sold.

foehn (FOHN)   A dry, warm wind that blows down a mountain.

glacier (GLAY-shuhr)   A large mass of ice that moves slowly over land.

legislature (LEJ-is-lay-chuhr)   A group of people who make and change laws.

prehistoric (pree-his-TOR-ik)   Existing in times before people wrote down history.

Fast Facts

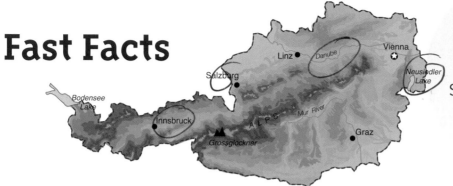

Austria is divided into nine provinces: Burgenland, Carinthia, Lower Austria, Salzburg, Styria, Tirol, Upper Austria, Vienna (the city), and Vorarlberg.

Austria's capital and largest city, Vienna, lies on the banks of the Danube River.

Austria's longest river is the Danube. It starts in Germany and runs through eight countries on its way to the Black Sea. It flows 217 miles (350 km) through the northern part of the country.

Mountains cover three-quarters of Austria's land. The most majestic of these are the Alps. Austria's tallest mountain is Grossglockner, located in the Central Alps. It is 12,457 feet (3,797 m) above sea level.

Austria's flag is made up of three horizontal stripes of equal width. In the center is one white stripe with a red stripe above and below.

In Austria, 73.6 percent of the people are Roman Catholic, 4.7 percent are Protestant, 4.2 percent are Muslim, 3.5 percent are other religions, 2 percent do not specify a religion, and 12 percent of the people do not follow a religion.

Austria uses the euro as its national currency. In May 2006, one euro equaled about $1.28 in the United States.

Austria's government is a republic. The president is the head of state and commander in chief of the armed forces. The people elect the president for a six-year term. The president appoints a chancellor, who serves for four years.

As of July 2006, there were 8,192,880 people living in Austria.

German is Austria's official language. It is spoken by about 98 percent of Austrians.

Proud to Be Austrian

Empress Maria Theresa (1717–1780)

Empress Maria Theresa is remembered today as the "Mother of Austria." This is not just because she had sixteen children! She was also a fine leader who made many positive changes in Austria for her citizens. But during her time, women were not permitted to inherit power in European kingdoms. Only men had that right. Her father Emperor Charles VI wanted to make sure the Habsburg family's rule continued after his death. With no sons, he wanted his eldest daughter, Maria Theresa, to inherit his throne. He passed a special law that allowed her to take over the empire after he died. She proved to be a wise leader. Under her rule, roads were built, an army was created, and a public school system was put in place. The Empress was also merciful. She ended the practice of torture and the execution of prisoners convicted of serious crimes. Maria Theresa's reign lasted for forty years from 1740 to 1780.

Wolfgang Amadeus Mozart (1756–1791)

From an early age Mozart performed for emperors and kings. This is because he was a genius who wrote his first piece of music at age five. He had perfect pitch and a fantastic memory. He was born in Salzburg. His father

Leopold, a highly skilled musician, recognized his son's talent and trained him. By age eight, Mozart had composed his first symphony. At twelve, he wrote an opera. During his short life he wrote more than six hundred pieces of music. Although he is honored today, he was not well treated during his adult life. He was paid poorly by his employers and often overlooked in favor of German and Italian composers. He died a poor man at the age of 35. Today the world still enjoys his brilliant talent.

Arnold Schwarzenegger (1947–)

Arnold Schwarzenegger was born in Thal, Austria. He was an excellent athlete as a boy. As a young adult, he became famous as a bodybuilder. He won the Mr. Universe title five times and the Mr. Olympia title seven times. He moved to the United States in 1968 and became a U.S. citizen in 1983. Hollywood liked his muscular appearance and Schwarzenegger got roles in many popular movies such as *Conan the Barbarian*, *The Terminator*, *True Lies*, and *Kindergarten Cop*. Schwarzenegger served on the President's Council on Physical Fitness from 1990–1993. In recent years he has become an investor in real estate and restaurants. He has also been active in politics. He was elected governor of California in 2003.

Find Out More

Books

Look What Came from Austria by Kevin A. Davis. Franklin Watts, Danbury, CT, 2002.

Who Was Wolfgang Amadeus Mozart? by Yona Zeldis McDonough. Grosset and Dunlap, New York, 2003.

Web Sites*

Academic Kids.com: Austria

http://academickids.com/encyclopedia/a/au/austria.html

Provides quick facts on Austria, including history, politics, geography, culture, and holidays.

National Geographic Kids News: Flying Horses: The Amazing Lipizzaners of Austria

http://news.nationalgeographic.com/kids/2005/10/horses.html

Gives a complete background of these magnificent acrobats, with links and tour schedules.

Saint Nicholas Center for Kids: Austria

http://stnicholas.kids.us/Brix?pageID=80

Tells how the saint is honored throughout Austria and how children prepare for his arrival.

*All Internet sites were available and accurate when sent to press.

Index

Page numbers for illustrations are in **boldface.**

About the Author

Deborah Grahame worked for many years as a book editor and freelance writer before becoming a children's book author. Learning about Austria's mountainous land brought to mind Deborah's childhood holidays in New York's Catskills and New Hampshire's White Mountains. Learning about Austria's wonderful food helped her recall her mom's famous goulash. Deborah's favorite Austrian composer is Mozart and her favorite Austrian beverage is coffee.

Deborah has also written *Sweden* for the Discovering Cultures series. She lives in southeastern Connecticut.